£5.50

Contents

Illustrated and designed by Arkadia Illustration and Design, London.

Published by Grandreams Limited
Jadwin House,
205/211 Kentish Town Road,
London, NW5 2JU.

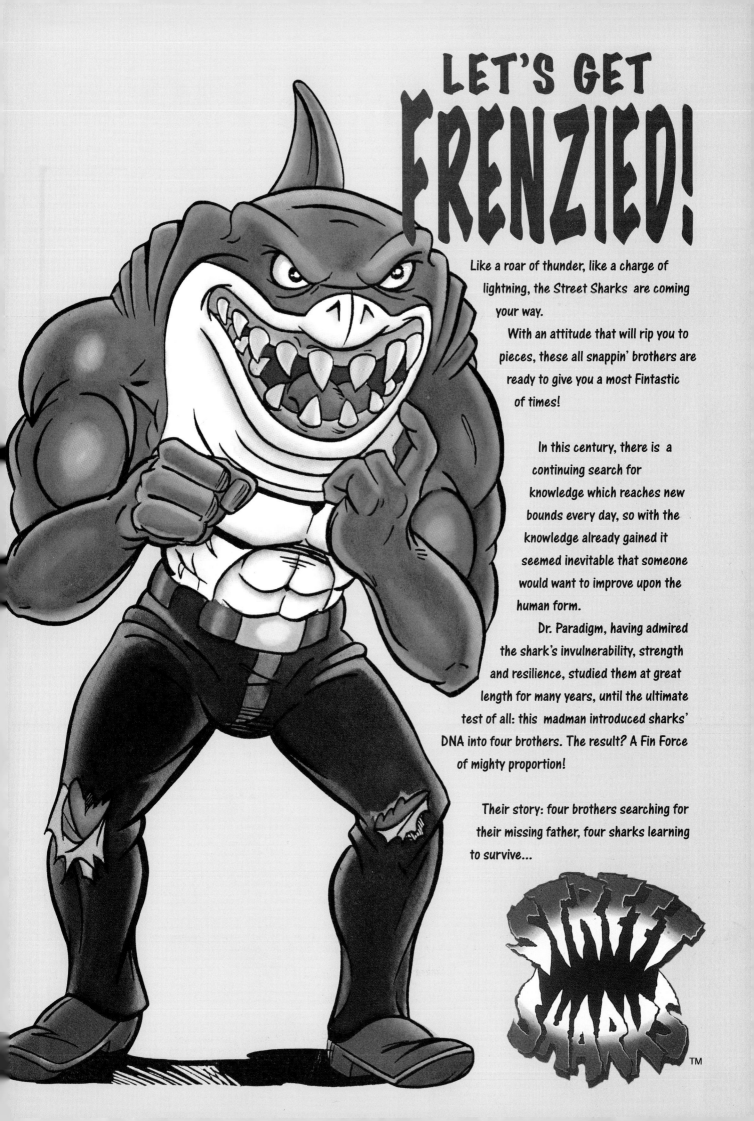

The Beginning...

It was a dark night and Dr. Paradigm was alone in an old abandoned science lab on the far side of town.

Locked away from the outside world he carefully studied the control panels in front of him.

Meanwhile, outside a dark figure was making his way through the surrounding fence and foliage to see what the Doctor was up to.

"Paradigm!" cried the figure as he entered the lab. "What are you doing?"

Paradigm turned away from the console and stared at the face of his old work colleague.

"I.." he started, "...am creating new life. I am recreating life forms to be even greater than their original form."

Dr Robert Bolton

shadows.

"Ah! Boys, if you'd like to follow me in, I'll show you where he is."

Dr. Paradigm lifted his arm to put it around John's shoulder when John suddenly noticed what was on Dr. Paradigm's wrist.

"That's Dad's watch!" cried out John. "He wouldn't part from that, Mum gave it to him."

Paradigm pulled away as the brothers began to close in on him.

"Boys, boys, boys. Calm down. Let me introduce you to some friends of mine."

Out of the shadow came two large, lumbering forms, a large mutated swordfish and alongside him a giant mutated lobster.

The brothers' faces became filled with horror. "They're not real!" they whimpered.

"Oh! They are real, boys. They are very real all right," smirked Paradigm.

"Tie the boys up and if they try to escape, you know what to do," barked Paradigm to his willing henchmen as they bundled the boys into the abandoned lab.

Inside the lab the boys were strapped down on metal trolleys.

"Boys, you should be proud. You, like your father, are about to be changed. You will become free of all the ills that mankind suffers." Paradigm walked over to a console and began to flick switches and turn dials.

"You won't get away with this!" shouted Coop, the youngest of the Bolton brothers.

Paradigm looked at the boys and smiled. "I remember someone else saying that," and flicked a switch.

Four hypodermic syringes descended from the ceiling over the bodies of the Bolton boys.

"Inside those syringes is the best thing that could ever happen to you," continued Paradigm. "From the ultimate predator, shark DNA, and once mixed with your own, all your worries will be gone."

"I think they'll just be starting!" muttered John as the syringe entered his arm.

Paradigm stared down at the lifeless form of the brothers.

"Dead, just like the others. The serum must have been too strong." He turned to his mutant Seavites. "Get rid of their bodies, they're no use to me now."

9

Slobster and Slash, as the Doctor had nicknamed the two mutants, picked up the now lifeless Bolton brothers and dumped them near an outlet pipe outside the labs.

"They'll be washed out to sea," hissed Slobster. "No one will see."

The dawn began to light the sky with pinks and reds as the sun began to rise over Fisson city. People began to get up just like any other day, unaware of the atrocities that had gone on the night before.

Lying on a beach on the outskirts of town lay four lifeless forms, washed there by water from an outlet.

Any passer-by would have assumed them to be four students sleeping off a good night out.

"Oh! My head!" muttered one of the forms as he slowly began to get up. His fellow sleepers also began to rise, clutching their heads.

"What happened? I feel like I've been hit by a cement truck."

"Me too. What did that Paradigm guy do?"

"Don't worry about that," whimpered Coop. "My stomach thinks there's a famine going on."

The four brothers got up and slowly limped along in the direction that the smell of fried onions and burgers was emanating from.

"Mmmm! That's better," mumbled Coop in between the bites of his burger.

The brothers continued to stuff their faces full of burgers topped with fried onions and mustard.

"Mama Mia!" whistled the burger bar vendor. "I have never seen anyone eat so fast, you have already had six each!"

"Mmmm!" mumbled John. "I don't know what's wrong with me but...I..I" but he started to splutter and

wheeze.

John felt as if his head was splitting open and his eyes were bulging. His head began to ache and his body began to grow.

"AAAAGH!" he cried. "What's happening to me?" John put his head in his hands.

"Urrrgh!" he screamed.

After the pain subsided John looked up at his brothers. They were different.

"Bro's!" he cried.

There in front of him were three shark-like figures. "What happened to you guys?" he simpered.

"Us!" said one of his brothers. "Look at you. You're just as sharky as us!"

"Sharky?" replied John "We're sharks!"

"Yes," said Coop. "We're sharks on land. Street Sharks!"

Their story continues...

Ripster ™

Age: 21
Hobbies: Pool and surfing
Fave music: Rock 'n' roll
Fave transport: Rip-Rider
Fave food: Toasters, microwaves and kipper burgers
Fave saying: "Let's get the Fin out of here!"

Ripster is the oldest of the four brothers and the leader of the pack.

Always in control of the situation, Ripster is relentless in his search for his father and for the truth about Dr. Paradigm.

Ripster has a double major in biology and engineering, which helps the brothers to understand their father's research and that of Dr Paradigm.

Before he was changed into half man, half shark, Ripster had plans to join a rock and roll band and to tour the country, later joining his father in his research for a better understanding of marine biology.

Having had his plans dashed, Ripster has stood up to that fact that his future won't be as he planned it. He hides his heartache and continues to be a great support to his younger brothers.

Jab™

Age: 20
Hobbies: Surfing and weight lifting
Fave music: Jazz
Fave transport: Jet pack
Fave food: Steel girders and prawn cocktails
Fave saying: "Shark Dive"

Jab is the most temperamental of the brothers - he can lose his temper at the drop of a Seavite.

But when he's not flaring up, Jab is the most good-natured of the sharks and the most lovable.

Jab loves to hurl insults at the Seavites who he feels most deserve a good fryin'.

Being the hot-head of the group can sometimes mean he gets the boys into more trouble than they want. In dangerous situations, Jab loves to find the easiest solution to the job which can mean he often bites off more than he can chew.

He has the ability to head butt his enemies with his hammer-head. That's when he's not hurling insults at them!

Jab is a business partner with Brandon Bends-Banner in the comic shop called "Suspended Reality". He and Bends have been good friends for many years, hanging out together and being real surfing brothers. Since Jab's change into a Street Shark, Bends and Jab's friendship has changed. Jab realises he and his brothers need to rely more and more on Bends for help and protection.

Streex ™

Age: 18
Hobbies: Surfing and roller-blading
Fave music: West Coast rock
Fave transport: Fin-line skates
Fave food: Toasters and tuna steak burgers
Fave saying: "Jawsome dudes!"

Streex is a ladies' man, or so he thinks! He loves to flirt and show off his Shark features, but he is yet to find a lady who finds a Tiger Shark attractive!

Streex is the most street-wise of the sharks, although this sometimes goes to his head.

He's always ready to go into action whatever the cost. And when danger threatens the lives of his brothers, he is more than willing to zoom in on his 'Fin-line skates'.

Before his change, Streex was going to enter the L.A. Street-hop roller blade competition. Now that he's a Street Shark he has put that idea on the back boiler as he feels that finding his father and keeping an eye on Dr. Paradigm is much more important.

Streex can be a little hot-headed at times, but with his older brother Ripster to keep him in check, things are just going 'Fintastically'!

Streex has retractable claws and with his tiger-like nature, the Seavites better watch out!

Big Slammu ™

Age: 16
Hobbies: American football
Fave music: Heavy rock
Fave transport: Shark Cruiser
Fave food: Anchovy pie
Fave saying: "Seismic slammin'!"

Big Slammu is the youngest of the brothers, a real gentle giant.

He thought the change he and his brothers went through was the coolest rush he had ever had!

Because of Slammu's size and strength, he can sometimes break things without meaning to. He is quite unaware at times of how strong he is and doesn't quite believe in himself enough.

Slammu wanted to be a champion football player and he sees no reason why he can't be, even if nobody wants to play with him anymore. The brothers have banned Slammu from playing football as he has caused too many accidents.

Slammu misses his father the most and cannot understand why he would want to leave him and his brothers. Ripster is Slammu's role model, although his grades have never followed suit.

Lovable Slammu is naive and sensitive, he greatly loves his brothers and hates to see anyone in pain. The youngest brother, he is willing to share everything and cannot bear to see anyone go without.

His greatest power is his "Seismic slam" which he does by slamming his fists against the ground creat- ·ing a mini earthquake.

Dr. Bolton™

Age: No data
Occupation: Scientist
Major Fields: Marine biology and bio-engineering

Dr. Robert Bolton is the Street Sharks' father. His disappearance is a complete mystery to both his sons and his old assistant Lena Mack.

Dr. Bolton has always studied hard to find the answers to the world's hunger and health problems. He felt that studying the DNA of marine life would solve his problems.

Always a good father, Dr. Bolton encouraged his sons to study hard and play hard. He is especially proud of John/Ripster, who gained a double major in biology and engineering, and had hoped that father and son would be able to study together.

Nobody knows what Dr. Bolton's last study was on, apart from that it involved marine DNA and a strange yellow substance that was found in the doctor's lab after he disappeared.

The doctor's lab has had a few visitors but it is believed from clues left behind that the doctor is alive and has been visiting the place. The mystery continues.

PUZZLERS
Goodie or Baddie?

Add a letter to each of the three letter words below to make a new word. Is it the name of a Street Shark or Seavite?

A creature that lays eggs	B	I	D	
Throw it to get a number	D	C	E	
To go round and round	S	I	N	
They are in the night sky	T	A	R	
Very big	A	L	L	
A large plant	T	R	E	
You run in it	A	C	E	

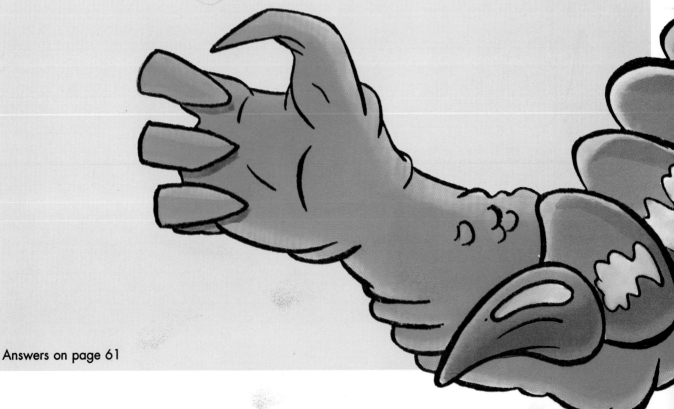

Answers on page 61

PUZZLERS
Odd Man Out

Listed below are the names of the Street Sharks™ and friends! Unmuddle the names and you will see an interloper in the list. But who?

1) HSSAL

2) PIRETSR

3) DNNOABR NSDBE-NNBARE

4) ENLA KCMA

5) GIB MMUASL

6) EERXTS

7) BJA

Answers on page 61.

PUZZLERS

The Number's Up!

The Street Sharks are on a mission. They have been told by their friend Lena Mack that Dr. Paradigm is planning something diabolical, so to make sure he won't get very far Jab has suggested going to take a look in the doctor's lab.

To get into Dr. Paradigm's lab, the Street Sharks need to break the code to the lab's keypad. Ripster was able to work out a few of the numbers, but can you help him to work out the rest?

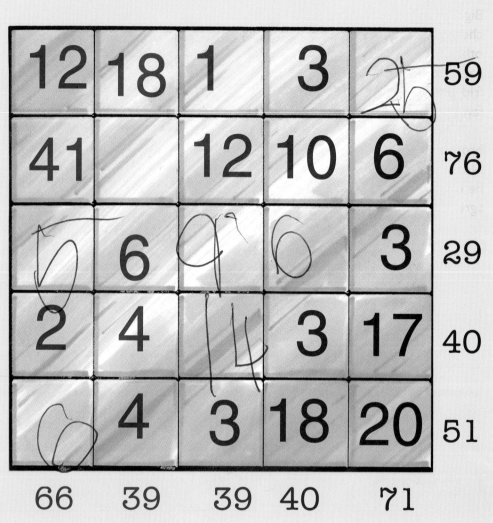

12	18	1	3		59
41		12	10	6	76
	6			3	29
2	4		3	17	40
	4	3	18	20	51
66	39	39	40	71	

When you have all the numbers in the keypad, look at the code below and highlight the keypad numbers above that will enable the Street Sharks' ENTRY.

Remember that A = 1, B = 2 so E = ?

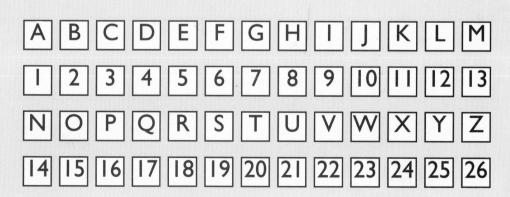

A	B	C	D	E	F	G	H	I	J	K	L	M
1	2	3	4	5	6	7	8	9	10	11	12	13
N	O	P	Q	R	S	T	U	V	W	X	Y	Z
14	15	16	17	18	19	20	21	22	23	24	25	26

Answers on page 61.

PUZZLERS

A Piece of the Pie!

Big Slammu likes nothing better than to chomp down on a slice of anchovy pie. The other day he decided he'd treat himself and have a small snack, but upon opening the fridge, he found only one slice of his favourite snack left.

Now Big Slammu is the youngest brother and also the most generous. Not wishing to let his brothers feel left out, he offered to share it and all of them readily agreed.

How will Slammu split the piece of pie equally between himself and his three brothers?

Answers on page 61.

A LITTLE BIT OF ACTION!

PUZZLERS

What's a Shark's Favourite Hobby?

```
C Z V N E D D N A T T Y Y
A A A A A A V B S J R S M
A S R S B B A N N B K S E
Q W X R A J Q A O Q U R O
A A I W A J E A M L L A L
T H W A W A C S R R R S P
A B S S S J A J A B E B M
C Q W R X J V B M H G B T
N M R W J R Z G M K L O E
A J W L Q Z W J R R S S Z
F I A U Y A Y R L J U B A
U S R R J J V S X M N B A
Q R L R A R W C X A U I O
F J T Y W J W S S S R R O
A I I A X A E J A A A S P
H B J U R S I A J B B V W
C N A N S L K Y A M V C W
Q T K B Q A W R K M K B Y
A B R J R S A R S R R J L
L E M N Z A X S A A A B A
A B R A A R A Z A C V T K
I S O J A J L R J J S R A
U S P L R B Y Y T I J A Y
O J A Q A S U W Q J O I T
E E W A A E E J J B S S N
P A L N A R A T N M D D M
A A M A R A A S J J R J O
L B S J X X Y S U I P R Y
V W Q A R W Q R A R O R W
A L A E A J A B S J M J A
O I K M T O P U A O P N Q
```

Hidden in the grid on the left is a Street Shark's favourite hobby. To find out what it is, shade in the boxes with the first letters of the Street Sharks names in. Two boxes are shaded in already for you.

Example:

R ipster

B ig Slammu

S treex

J ab

PUZZLERS

A BIG SECRET

The Street Sharks have been sent a secret message by a friend. Help them to find out what the message is and who is trying to warn them, by deciphering the code. Good luck!

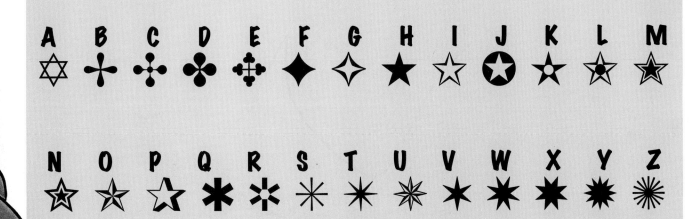

A B C D E F G H I J K L M

N O P Q R S T U V W X Y Z

Answers on page 61.

Recipe pages

Shark Bites

The Street Sharks enjoy a good bite or two and in between surfing, sharking and chasing Dr. Paradigm the boys like to enjoy some of their favourite nibbles.

Below are a few of the Sharks favourites. Ask a grown-up to help you make a few and have a feeding frenzy!

TUNA STEAK BURGERS

(This recipe needs a grown-up to do all of the cooking)

TUNA FISH
TABASCO SAUCE
OLIVE OIL
A SMALL ONION
ONE EGG
SOME LIGHTLY SEASONED FLOUR
MAYONNAISE AND GRUYERE CHEESE SLICES

1. Put your tuna fish in a bowl and mash to a pulp. Add the chopped onion.

2. Put a little tabasco sauce in the bowl to flavour. Add the egg and mix well.

3. Take a small handful of the tuna. Make a burger shape and roll in the flour.

4. Gently fry your burgers in olive oil. Drain and then serve in a sesame bun with a little mayonnaise and the cheese. Jawsome!

SPICY TUNA SANDWICH SPREAD

TABASCO SAUCE
A TIN OF TUNA IN BRINE
BLACK PEPPER
SPRING ONIONS
MAYONNAISE

1. Get a grown-up to lightly chop the spring onions.

2. Drain the tuna fish and put in a bowl.

3. Add mayonnaise to the tuna and mix well till the tuna is covered.

4. Add a touch of tabasco and black pepper to the tuna.

5. Add the spring onions and serve.

SURF BOARD RIDERS

BANANAS
WHIPPED CREAM
PEACH AND APPLE SLICES
TOFFEE SAUCE

1. Peel your banana and have a grown-up cut a slit in the banana, end to end, but do not split the banana.

2. Insert your slices of fruit into the banana standing up to look like surfers.

3. Have the grown-up microwave your surfboard till just warm.

4. Add the banana to the whipped cream which is pretending to be waves.

5. Dribble toffee sauce over the surfers for extra yummyness. Enjoy.

PRAWN COCKTAILS

PRAWNS
MAYONNAISE
CAYENNE PEPPER
SHREDDED LETTUCE
A LEMON

1. Put some mayonnaise in a bowl and mix in some cayenne pepper.

2. Put your shredded lettuce in a serving bowl.

3. Add your prawns to the mayonnaise and then pour on top of your lettuce.

4. Squeeze the juice of the lemon on top of your prawns and serve.

DEEP SEA DESSERT

DIGESTIVE BISCUITS
LIME GREEN JELLY
BLUEBERRY JELLY
FISH SHAPED JELLY SWEETS
WHIPPED CREAM
A LARGE CLEAR GLASS BOWL

1. Crush the digestive biscuits until they are crumbs and then press them tightly into the bottom of the bowl.

2. Make up the green jelly and then pour it on top of the biscuits. Add a few of the sweets. Leave to set.

3. Make the blueberry jelly and then pour it on top of the green jelly. Add the rest of the sweets, leave to set.

4. Squirt the whipped cream on top of the blue jelly and your dessert will be ready. The deep sea, complete with fish and rolling waves!

(If you don't like whipped cream, allow some ice-cream to slightly melt. Whip it to look like waves and pour it on top of your dessert instead of the cream.)

SEAWEED SHAKE

VANILLA ICE-CREAM
MILK
GREEN FOOD COLOURING
GREEN SWEET SHOE LACES

1. Get a grown-up to put a few spoons of ice-cream and milk in a food blender and whip the two together.

2. Add a little food colouring and then pour into a tall glass.

3. Add a few strands of the sweet shoe laces to make strands of seaweed and serve.

Bends™

Name: Brandon Bends-Banner
Age: 19
Hobbies: Surfing and gadget making
Fave music: Grunge
Fave transport: Van
Fave food: Ketchup and jelly sandwich

Brandon Bends-Banner, or Bends for short, has always been a friend to the Street Sharks even before they changed. He was most shocked by the change and was a close friend to the boys' father, Dr. Bolton, as well. Because of what has happened to his friends, he is willing to help the Street Sharks stop Dr Paradigm.

He is the eyes and ears of the Street Sharks and hides them in the basement of his comic book shop "Suspended Reality".

Bends is a mechanical engineering student which helps him to practice his hobby of making all sorts of gadgets. He uses this hobby to help his friends by building weapons and vehicles to use against Dr. Piranoid.

Bends is closest to Jab and feels protective of his friends, although he isn't too overprotective.

He has a cool head but can be a little clutter-brained at times. Bends plans to create the ultimate gadget that no one will be able to do without and will make him rich. He is yet to figure out though what this gadget will be, but he is getting **a lot of practise with the Street** Sharks around.

Lena™

Name: Lena Mack
Job: Lab technician
Nationality: African American
Fave food: Nothing fishy

Lena worked for Dr. Bolton before his disappearance. She was also close to the brothers and still is. She has a soft spot for Big Slammu.

Since Dr. Bolton's disappearance and the brothers' transformation, she has been working for Dr. Paradigm so that she can keep a close eye on him and keep the Street Sharks informed.

Lena's main field of study is bioengineering and she hopes that the studies she partakes in will help to eradicate hunger and illness.

She does not believe that Dr. Paradigm is up to any good and strongly believes he was the one who had the boys infected with shark DNA.

She hopes to find a cure for the Street Sharks but at the moment there is no hope without Dr. Bolton.

Lena feels that Dr. Bolton would be proud of his sons, who have faced their dilemma with strength and humour and hopes one day all will be well.

TRIVIA QUIZ

Let's see if you dudes have been paying attention to what's been going on!

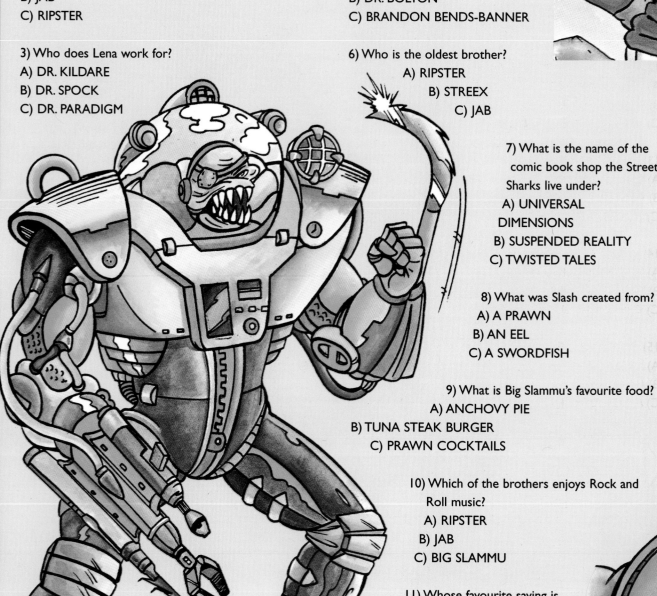

1) How many brothers are there in the Street Sharks?
A) TWO
B) FOUR
C) THREE

2) Which Street Shark believes he is a ladies' man?
A) STREEX
B) JAB
C) RIPSTER

3) Who does Lena work for?
A) DR. KILDARE
B) DR. SPOCK
C) DR. PARADIGM

4) Who is Dr Paradigm's alter ego?
A) WHELK MAN
B) PARASITE FEATURES
C) DR. PIRANOID

5) Who is the Street Sharks' father?
A) DR. PARADIGM
B) DR. BOLTON
C) BRANDON BENDS-BANNER

6) Who is the oldest brother?
A) RIPSTER
B) STREEX
C) JAB

7) What is the name of the comic book shop the Street Sharks live under?
A) UNIVERSAL DIMENSIONS
B) SUSPENDED REALITY
C) TWISTED TALES

8) What was Slash created from?
A) A PRAWN
B) AN EEL
C) A SWORDFISH

9) What is Big Slammu's favourite food?
A) ANCHOVY PIE
B) TUNA STEAK BURGER
C) PRAWN COCKTAILS

10) Which of the brothers enjoys Rock and Roll music?
A) RIPSTER
B) JAB
C) BIG SLAMMU

11) Whose favourite saying is "Jawsome dudes!"?
A) STREEX
B) BIG SLAMMU
C) BENDS

17) Which type of DNA was accidentally injected into Dr. Paradigm?
A) PIRANHA
B) SHARK
C) EEL

18) Who makes Seismic Slams?
A) BIG SLAMMU
B) RIPSTER
C) JAB

19) What's Bends' favourite hobby?
A) MAKING CAKES
B) MAKING MODELS
C) MAKING GADGETS

12) What nationality is Lena Mack?
A) INDIAN AMERICAN
B) FRENCH AMERICAN
C) AFRICAN AMERICAN

20) Who has the sixth sense for danger?
A) JAB
B) BIG SLAMMU
C) RIPSTER

13) Who rides in the Shark Cruiser?
A) BIG SLAMMU
B) RIPSTER
C) BENDS

21) What city do the Street Sharks live in?
A) FISSION
B) FUSION
C) FASHION

14) Where do the Street Sharks like to hang out the most?
A) THE LOCAL HEALTH CLUB
B) THE LOCAL LIBRARY
C) THE LOCAL BURGER STAND

22) How did John know something was wrong with his father when he saw Dr. Paradigm?
A) HE HAD HIS FATHER'S TOUPEE
B) HE HAD HIS FATHER'S SHOES
C) HE HAD HIS FATHER'S WATCH

15) What is West Coast Rock?
A) A DANCE
B) A DRINK
C) A TYPE OF SURF MUSIC

23) What is Slammu's favourite hobby?
A) AMERICAN FOOTBALL
B) SWIMMING
C) SURFING

16) What is Doctor Bolton's first name?
A) FRED
B) JOHN
C) ROBERT

24) Which Seavite can bore through steel?
A) SLOBSTER
B) JAB
C) SLASH

25) Who saved Jab and Streex from being washed away?
A) BIG SLAMMU'S BROTHER
B) BIG SLAMMU'S FRIEND
C) BIG SLAMMU'S MATH TEACHER

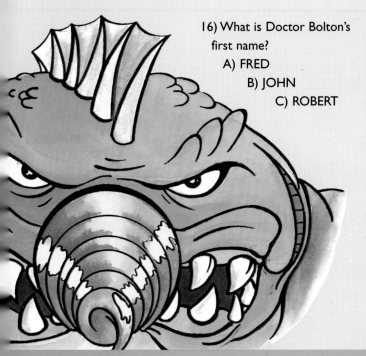

SHARK FACT ATTACK!

BODYWORK

Sharks vary in size from a mere 20cm (8ins) long, which is the lantern shark, to the whopping size of 12m (40ft) long, which is the whale shark, but on average, sharks are approximately less than a metre long.

Their skin is covered in small teeth-like implements called denticles, which give the skin a rough feel when stroked the wrong way. (That's only, of course, if you want to stroke one!)

Sharks need gills to breathe through and these supply them with a rich source of oxygen.

Some active sharks which swim near the surface of the sea like the white-tip, need a continual flow of water through their gills so they must swim without stopping, not even to sleep.

If these sharks do stop swimming, (whether they are trapped or just get tired!) the water flow stops and so does the oxygen supply, so the shark drowns!

A shark's insides are very similar to our own: they have a heart that pumps blood around the body, a stomach for digestion and a liver and kidneys for waste removal.

Some sharks have very small brains in comparison with their body size. For instance, some breeds of shark have the same size brain as a bird that is a tenth of their body size.

Ever since the film Jaws was released, sharks have been getting very bad press. They are portrayed as vicious killers who will silently swim through the water to eat an innocent swimmer or surfer.

The fact that you are more likely to die in a car crash than be eaten by a shark doesn't seem to change people's view.

What people don't realise is that even though sharks are skilled predators, many of the 375 or so species of shark are so shy that it is very difficult to find them, let alone be attacked by one.

Many shark species prefer warm water, such as off the Florida coast, but the largest concentration of sharks is around the Australian coast.

TEETH

Because of their diets, sharks rely heavily upon their teeth.

Sharks have two rows of chompers in their mouths. Some of these teeth are so sharp they can bite through a car license plate!

Unlike us, sharks are able to replace any of the teeth

they lose, but because of their tough diets this can mean them getting through thousands of teeth throughout their lifetime.

How can they do this? Easy when you're a shark, and all without the aid of a dentist, not that you'll find that many in the sea!

Sharks' teeth continue to grow through their lives and when a tooth in the front row of the shark's mouth becomes worn or lost, a tooth behind pushes forward to replace it.

Each tooth forms in the shark's gums and rotates forwards as it grows until it drops out, hence the fact you will never see a shark with no teeth and no toothache!

FOOD

Sharks will eat anything they can find in the sea. Their main diet is fish and squid but this can be interspersed with sea birds and turtles.

Some sharks have been known to eat other smaller sharks and sea mammals such as dolphins or seals. But the strangest part of a shark's diet is his continuous interest in junk. Not junk food but *junk*, rubbish.

The sea is heavily polluted with all sorts of rubbish and sharks have a habit of eating anything that is floating around.

One shark was found to have eaten several license plates, a false arm and some tin cans.

Sharks have also been known to have eaten plastic carrier bags, books, hub-caps, nuts and bolts and a shop mannequin!

Not exactly what you would call a healthy diet!

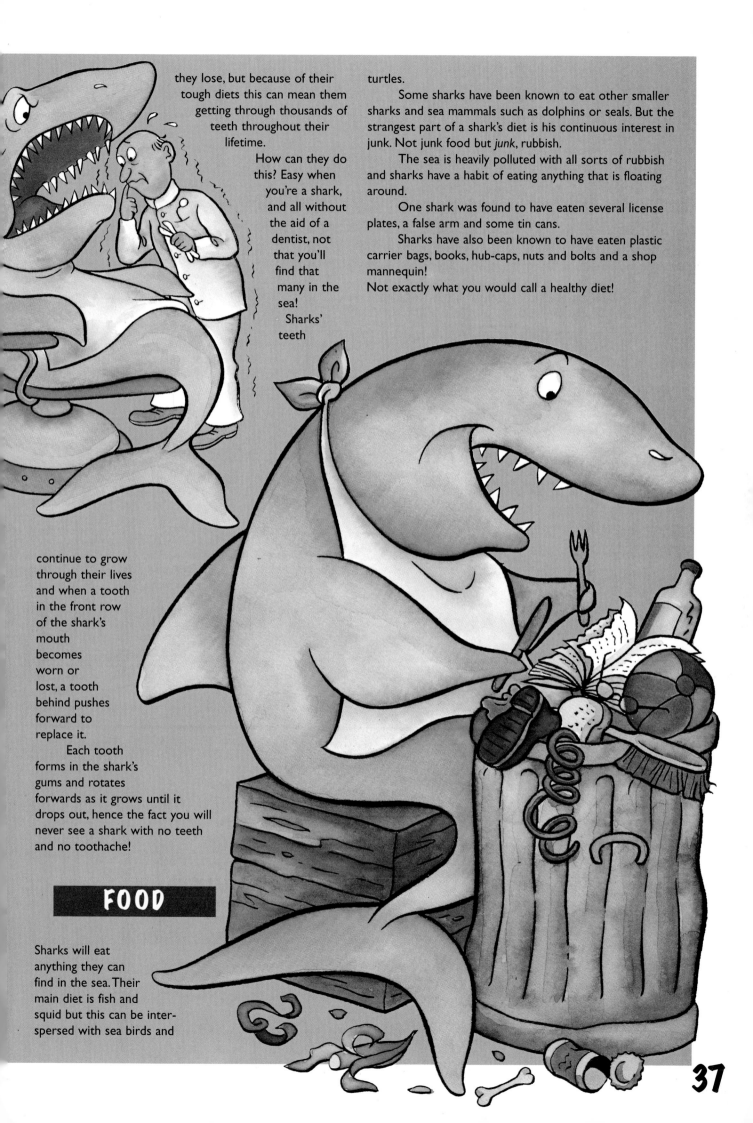

SIXTH SENSE

Sharks are stealthy predators and to help them catch their meals they have adapted themselves to gain a sixth sense.

We have five senses: sight, hearing, taste, touch and smell. Sharks have a sixth sense which is the ability to pick up and decipher the

small electrical pulses that are generated by a fish or anything else that gives off vibrations in the water.

Sharks are able to pick up these vibrations along a sensitive part of their body called the lateral line.

These lateral lines run down either side of the shark's body and each line is made up of small canals with tiny pores. Beneath these pores are cells with microscopic hairs. These hairs pick up the vibrations and send messages to the brain.

Sometimes these messages can be deciphered incorrectly. Instead of the shark thinking that he's about

to bite a fish, he could be about to bite a swimmer. Swimmers give off the same signals as large fish and this fact can be attributed to some shark attacks.

FRIENDS

Sharks would never like to be thought of as an unfriendly bunch of guys!

They have in reality quite a few friends, especially two close ones called remoras and pilot fish.

Remoras have found that sharks make a great bus service, even if they do have long waits and then two come along at the same time!

Remoras have large suckers on the top of their heads which enable them to attach themselves to the underside of the shark. There they are able to move through vast areas of the sea, heavily protected. Using the shark as a bodyguard, remoras are allowed to live unmolested, as well as

having a good source of leftovers - sharks are not very tidy eaters!

In return for protection and transportation remoras remove unwanted parasites from the shark's body, a service which the shark finds invaluable.

Pilots also use the sharks as bodyguards and because of their dark markings are able to hide in the shark's shadow.

Because of their ability to move quite quickly, they don't make it to become shark food.

Protected from their enemy, these fish are able to snap up any suitable nibbles.

REPELLENT

Researchers abroad have tried to study ways of making sure that swimmers are never attacked by sharks.

One group found that sharks will not swim through electrical currents. This may be because it effects their navigation.

An electric pulse was used to block a tunnel and although the shark would not have been able to see the electric field, the shark would not swim through the tunnel until the pulse was turned off.

Another study on sharks found that if a person was floating on a large inflatable bag a shark would not attack him because it could neither see arms or legs nor sense electrical pulses.

But the most natural of repellents has been found to be a milky secretion made by a fish called the Moses Sole. When attacked the fish secretes the milky fluid which makes the shark spit it out.

scientists continue to study these mighty beasts, their understanding of sharks has lead them to believe that these animals are not just floating dustbins. They are *'Jawsome creatures'! of the deep.*

THE END

Sharks are hunted for many different reasons: from fear, for food, for cosmetics and for pleasure.

Shark oil has been used in cosmetics for many years, whereas their teeth and skin have been used for jewellery.

This continuous hunting has put some shark species on the endangered list. In Australia the Great White shark has become an endangered species and in South Africa shark hunting is banned.

A lot about sharks is still not known and as

PUZZLERS
Street Shark Wordsearch

Slobster has hidden the names of the Street sharks' friends and enemies.
Hunt in the wordsearch below and see if you can find them all.

```
A S L A S H E U W I Q D A S K D U W
R I P S T E R B N I I Q D A S K D S
S S D B K J E U W I Q D A S K B U L
L S D E K J E U A I Q D A S K I U A
O S D N K J E U W I Q D A S K G U M
B S D D K J E U W I Q D A S K D U M
S S D S K J E U R I S D A S K D U U
T S D H K J E U V I T D A S K D R W
E S D H K J D R P A R A D I G U M M
R S D H K J A B W D E A S K R U L L
A S D H K J E U M D E A S K D U E E
A S D H K J E U W I X D A S K D U N
D R B O L T O N W I Q M A C K D U A
```

RIPSTER
BIG SLAMMU
JAB
STREEX
DR. BOLTON
DR. PARADIGM
LENA MACK
BENDS
SLOBSTER
SLASH

Answers on page 61.

A Totally Electric Time

Dr. Paradigm was sitting in his lab downtown, staring idly at a tank that had a catfish swimming around in it.

"How can I stop those meddling sharks from spoiling my plans?" he cursed.

The catfish continued to swim, undaunted by the doctor's ranting.

"There should be an easy answer to this problem. I have to find a solution or I will never be able to succeed."

Paradigm picked up a pencil and started to stir the water in the tank that the catfish was in. It continued to swim undaunted.

Staring at the fish, Paradigm withdrew the pencil from the water. "You're a distant relative of these sharks, how would you stop them? Heh!" The fish continued to ignore him.

Lena Mack walked in. "Sorry to disturb you, Dr. Paradigm, but I've got those test results you wanted."

Lena walked over to the doctor and handed him the files she had brought in.

Paradigm took the files without even looking up. "MMmmm. Thank you, Miss Mack, that will be all," he muttered and continued to stare at the catfish.

Lena shrugged her shoulders and left the doctor to his thoughts.

Paradigm got up and walked over to the window. Outside two engineers in overalls were fixing some cabling and passing it underground and a woman was walking her dog on the grass opposite.

Paradigm could see Lena leaving to go and get some lunch.

Suddenly, the dog became loose from its lead and ran across the road towards the two engineers. Distracted by the commotion, one of the engineers dropped the cabling and began trying to catch the dog.

Paradigm continued to watch as now both engineers, the woman who owned the dog and Lena chased it to try and catch it.

Meanwhile the cabling that had been dropped for some reason began to spark and fizz with an electrical current.

The dog changed course and escaped past the two engineers towards the electric cabling. It then stopped short, refusing to jump over the cabling or walk around it.

One of the engineers caught up with the dog and handed it to his owner. The other engineer went off supposedly to turn the power off.

Paradigm stared at the cabling. The dog had refused to go any further when it saw the electric cabling sparking with life. Had it become scared or had it sensed danger?

Paradigm turned away from the window and stared at the catfish who was continuing to swim unaffected by the whole affair outside. "That's it!" he cried.

Rushing into another lab, Paradigm picked up some electric cabling and set to work on his plan.

Some hours later, Paradigm had what he wanted and took the device with him back to where the catfish was happily swimming around in the tank.

Lowering one wire into one side of the tank and another down the other side, Paradigm picked up a small morsel of food and dropped it in one end of the tank.

Sensing a nibble the catfish started to sniff around the water, waving its head from side to side to try and find where the food was.

"Now!" said Paradigm. "Let's see if my theory is correct about this,"

The catfish now knew where the food was and began to swim to the

41

other end of the tank.

Paradigm switched on his device which sent an electric current through the water from wire to wire making an electric gate.

Immediately the catfish stopped swimming, as if sensing something was wrong.

"That's it! Sharks won't swim through electric currents. I now know how to stop those sharks."

Paradigm switched off the power and the catfish began to swim back up to the other end of the tank. Again

Paradigm switched on the power and again the catfish stopped swimming.

"Now, my little ankle biters. Now I have the power to stop you!"

Paradigm continued to switch the device on and off, watching the catfish try and swim towards the food without passing through the electric gateway without much success.

Meanwhile, down in the basement of the comic book store Suspended Reality, Bends was doing some much needed repairs on the Shark Cruiser.

Streex was looking at a magazine showing all the latest gear for roller-blading and Jab was taking a nap as usual.

Ripster and Big Slammu had

to get a feeling along his lateral line and when Ripster has a feeling, you know there's trouble brewing!

"I've got a feeli..." before Ripster could finish telling his brother how he felt, Slash's van came whizzing around a corner and drove straight past the brothers at high speed. "Whaaatt!"

Both brothers did a double take, then Slammu picked the trolley up and threw it in the back of the van. He jumped in alongside his brother,

replied Streex.

Slash was laughing to himself as he accelerated down the street. "Those sharks have fallen for the bait, Dr. Paradigm will be pleased!"

Ripster and Slammu continued to follow Slash's van which sped around corner after corner. Ripster had a hard time keeping up with the Seavite but his determination kept him going.

The Seavites' van continued to drive along the street at high speed,

gone out to the local supermarket to get some food, which in Slammu's belief was much needed. He had felt the fridge had been looking mighty empty recently and this worried him a lot!

"So, bro, that little lot should keep us going for a while!" said Ripster staring at the trolley piled high with food.

Slammu was pushing the laden trolley to the van when Ripster began

setting off in hot pursuit of the Seavite, Slash.

"What do you think he's up to?" asked Slammu.

"Haven't a clue, but you had better radio to the others, he seemed in a big hurry for something!" Slammu picked up the radio transmitter and called his two older brothers down in the basement.

"Don't worry, bro, we'll be with you in two flicks of a lemon sole's tail!"

then it turned into a tunnel. The Street Sharks followed into the darkness and came up in a disused baseball stadium.

There in the middle of the field was Slash's van, but no sign of Slash.

Ripster turned to Slammu. "Radio the others and tell them where we are. I think it's the old ArchAngels Stadium on Pit Street."

Slammu picked up the radio transmitter which had begun to spark and splutter with static out of the hand set.

"There's some kind of interference, I can't get through."

The lights of the stadium suddenly came on, blinding the sharks, and then followed the voice of Dr. Paradigm.

"Get ready, sharks, you're about to have a truly electrical time!"

As Ripster's eyes became accustomed to the bright lights, he saw that the whole stadium was covered in wires that criss-crossed over all the seats and across the field surrounding them.

Dr. Paradigm picked up a small hand-held device. "There'll be fish frying tonight, if I have my way!" he laughed hysterically and flicked a large switch on the hand-held device.

Power surged through the wires surrounding the Street Sharks, which began to glow with the heat.

"Ah oh, looks like trouble," muttered Slammu to his brother as a worried look crossed his face.

"Stay cool, don't worry, bro. It's not as bad as it looks."

As the cabling became charged with electricity it began to tighten slowly, trapping the two brothers.

In the van the radio receiver still sparked and spluttered, but Jab's voice could be heard through the static trying to get through. "Ripster, Slammu, bro's, are you there?"

In the Shark Cruiser Jab was still trying to raise his brothers on the radio. "Bro's, bro's, are you there?"

Bends was driving the Shark Cruiser which was speeding along when suddenly the lights began to go out in the buildings along the street.

"Heh! What's going on?" said Streex turning to Bends. "The power's going, all the buildings are losing power. You're the engineering dude. What's going on?"

Bends looked out of the window and could see that all the building lights were going off. People were coming out to see what was going on.

"Must be a power drain, someone has tapped into the electricity grid and is draining it of power."

Both Streex and Jab looked at each other, each coming to the same conclusion as the other.

"Wherever the power drain is I bet we'll find the bros," said Streex turning to Bends, "so step on it."

"And I bet that when we find the

bros, we'll find a speeding Seavite and a lot of trouble," ended Jab.

Bends pulled out a small device from the glove compartment and handed it to Jab. "Scan the area and see where the power drain is coming from."

Jab pulled up the aerial and stuck it out the window, twisting a dial. A small screen on the scanner came on and started to bleep. "There's a power surge in that direction," pointed Jab. "Near the old baseball stadium, it must be where all the power's going."

The Shark Cruiser sped off in the direction Jab had pointed, while more and more buildings began to go dark from losing power.

Meanwhile at the baseball stadium the wires were becoming more and more taut, trapping Ripster and Big Slammu. Both brothers had jumped back into the van to avoid being hit by the wire cabling.

"I am not swimming through that lot," Slammu muttered, looking nervously out of the windscreen.

"I don't want you to," Ripster replied. "We sharks don't like electricity, it stops electrical messages going to the brain and hurts our navigation systems. We would just get lost."

Dr. Paradigm was getting more and more excited by the minute. His plan to get rid of the Street Sharks seemed to be working and as soon as the last stretch of wire was charged with electricity, the two brothers would be fried.

Ripster grabbed his younger brother's hand tightly to calm him. His eyes scanned the stadium to see a way out of the situation.

"It's gonna be all right bro, there's still a lot of cabling to go."

Ripster continued to look around and then saw where all the cabling was coming from. Attached to the far wall of the stadium was a large fuse box.

In the hurry to attach the wiring, Dr. Paradigm had not noticed that the fuse box was right under a large water tower.

"Slammu! Slammu!" said Ripster excitedly. "I've got a plan and I need your help."

Both brothers jumped out of the van and ducked. The wire cabling above it began to fizz with energy. "We can't swim out but maybe we can slam out!"

Ripster explained he wanted some real seismic waves, powerful enough to topple the water tower. And as soon as the tower had toppled and the water had cut out the electricity supply, they would have to dive down or the cabling would give them a nasty shock or two.

Slammu lifted his hands above hid head and then crashed them down to the ground. "Seismic slam!" he cried.

The ground shook with the vibrations that emanated from Slammu's fists, again and again he pummelled the ground till the whole stadium shook.

The water tower first shook from side to side and then came crashing down. It covered the fuse box and then the cabling with water.

"Duck, bro!" screamed out Ripster as the cabling began to whip around the stadium.

Up in the observation tower above the stadium, Paradigm had been watching the goings on. His face began to fill with anger, his body started to shake and large, sharp teeth began to fill his mouth. Dr. Piranoid was coming!

"Nooo!" he cried as the tower toppled over into the stadium.

With the power short circuited the electricity supply was cut to the cabling. All that was left for it to do was fizz and spark.

Ripster and Slammu came up from underneath the van. The cabling lay limp on the ground and the pair began to weave their way over to the now fallen observation tower.

A slight whiff of charred fish began to greet the two brothers as they got closer to the rubble.

Suddenly out jumped Slash and Slobster, smoke coming from their slightly toasted bodies, each glowing red with heat.

"The cables are still hot!" cried Slobster. "No, you're joking!" replied Slash.

There was no sign of Dr. Piranoid.

The Shark Cruiser pulled up outside the stadium. Rubble littered the road where some of the old stadium had fallen.

"Slammu has definitely been here," said Jab turning to Bends. "No!" replied Bends. "What gave you that impression?"

Out of the entrance to the stadium charged Slobster and Slash, followed shortly by Ripster and Slammu. Both Seavites continued to charge down the street glowing red while Ripster and Slammu joined their brothers.

" What kept you bros?" asked Slammu.

"Lack of power," replied Ripster. "They just didn't have the energy to keep up with the electric dudes!" Jab, Streex and Bends gave Ripster a very strange look while Slammu burst out laughing.

PUZZLERS

True or False?

Jab is a hammer-head shark, an unusual but real name. Listed below are supposedly names of different species of shark. Can you tell which are true and which are made up?

	TRUE	FALSE
TIGER SHARK	☐	☐
RED SHARK	☐	☐
ISLE OF WIGHT SHARK	☐	☐
BLUE SHARK	☐	☐
DOCTOR SHARK	☐	☐
ELEPHANT SHARK	☐	☐
HORSE SHARK	☐	☐
NURSE SHARK	☐	☐
RED NOSE SHARK	☐	☐
WHALE SHARK	☐	☐
PORT JACKSON SHARK	☐	☐
SCREWDRIVER SHARK	☐	☐
BLACK TIP SHARK	☐	☐
DOLPHIN SHARK	☐	☐
DEMON SHARK	☐	☐
LEOPARD SHARK	☐	☐
SMELLY SHARK	☐	☐
ANGEL SHARK	☐	☐
HORN SHARK	☐	☐
HORSE SHARK	☐	☐
BEACH SHARK	☐	☐
LARGE SHARK	☐	☐
SNAKE SHARK	☐	☐
ZEBRA SHARK	☐	☐
PUZZLE SHARK	☐	☐
CROCODILE SHARK	☐	☐

Suspended Reality

The Street Sharks hide out in the basement of the comic book shop "SUSPENDED REALITY". How many words can you make out of the letters that make up the comic book shop's title? Only use each letter once per word and each word must be longer than four letters.

Here some the boys made up earlier.

1. SPEEDY
2. SPEND
3. DEADLY
4. RUSTY
5. TRAILS
6. SUSPEND

How many more can you find?

_____

_____

_____

_____

_____

_____

_____

_____

Answers on page 61.

Surf Buddies!

The rain spat heavily against the panes of glass as Bends and Jab leaned against a counter in the comic book shop they owned.

They were reading some new comics that had come in that day. They were all about a new super hero who roamed the beach saving people and stopping the bad guys polluting the beach. Both guys were really excited by what they were reading, especially when they found out their new hero surfed to save the heroine.

"Man, this rain is driving me crazy, all I want to do is go and surf!" lamented Bends, who had conveniently forgotten that he'd surfed all day yesterday and the day before.

"Yeah! You're right. This rain is ruining the surf, my fin is beginning to dry out!"

Downstairs Streex was cleaning his Fin-Line skates. They'd got covered in mud when he'd gone for a cruise that morning.

"Blast this rain! When will it stop? I need to go for a spin."

Ripster was teaching Big Slammu how to play chess and both sharks were having a great time.

"Just be patient, bro, it's only been raining a couple of hours. The weatherman said it would finish soon."

This made no impact whatsoever on Streex, who felt valuable skating time was being lost. He'd heard that the local surf shop had a new shop assistant who was a real surf chick and he felt she should be blessed with his sharkness!

Up in the shop the phone rang. It was Lena Mack, the Street Sharks' close friend and ally and she had news about Dr. Paradigm.

Jab answered the phone.

"Boys! He's up to something, he left the laboratory this morning with a fishtank that he had covered up."

"Don't worry," said Jab. "The bros and I will check it out. Do you know where he might be going? Have a look and see if he's got any other labs."

Lena said she would check and call them back while Jab went and told his brothers the news.

"MMmm," said Ripster. "I had a feeling today was going to be different."

"Really?" muttered Streex. "Will someone please tell me what is so suspicious about the old doc leaving his labs with a fish tank?"

Ripster and Jab both turned to their younger brother simultaneously.

"Because.." said Ripster, "..because he's obviously hiding something. Why would you take a fish tank away from one of the most expensive, fully-equipped lab and marine centres in the country, unless you were trying to hide something?"

"Ah!" replied Streex still not convinced by his brother's explanation, but he knew his brother had a sixth sense when it came to trouble and he'd never been wrong in the past.

Lena phoned back to say she'd found some invoices for the rental of a lab across town and that a package had

arrived this morning for Dr. Paradigm that had been flown in from the West Indies.

The brothers agreed to head across town to see if they could find the doctor.

Some hours later, having got lost several times, the brothers came across a large building that offered the rental of fully-equipped labs.

"This must be the place," muttered Jab. "Lena gave me the name of the building and this is it."

Slammu said he'd wait with the vehicles while his older brothers had a look around.

The reception area was empty and as the boys wandered through the building they found that empty, too. Each floor had a fully equipped lab, all with state-of-the-art equipment but no people. The place was deserted and it looked as if they had all left in a hurry.

"Where'd everyone go?" said Jab turning to Ripster. "Do you think someone knew we were coming?"

Ripster shrugged his shoulders. "Let's split up. We can cover more ground that way."

Ripster went to check the labs on the other floors and Jab and Streex went to check the basement.

Slammu was getting bored standing outside when he suddenly saw something move out of the corner of his eye in a window on the second floor.

"Slobster? No, no, maybe it's Slash? Oh maybe not." Whoever it was, he was going to follow them. They looked very suspicious to him.

Down in the cellar, Jab and Streex could hear a loud humming sound that was being made by large machinery. They could also hear some heavy cursing.

"Someone's down here, but who?" whispered Jab.

Jab indicated to Streex to see if he could find another way in, while Jab prepared to charge in through the doorway in front of him.

"1..2..3!" Jab charged through one doorway and Streex through another on the other side of the room.

There inside was Dr. Piranoid, fuming and cursing to his two henchmen, Slobster and Slash.

"Blast you!" he cursed "What do you mean, you've lost him? He couldn't have gone far."

At that moment he realised who else was in the room : Jab and Streex.

"Heh! Mollusc features and Seaweed breath! You miss us?"

"Blast it!" screamed Dr. Piranoid and lifted his right arm, firing a harpoon at Jab.

Slash started his nose whirring and charged towards Streex.

Jab ducked the harpoon that Dr. Piranoid had fired. He met the full onslaught of Slobster charging at him with his claws slamming open and shut.

"Come and get me, Ugleee!" he cried out.

Up on the roof, Ripster had found nothing and no one. Looking over the edge he could see where the Shark Cruiser and motorcycle were but no sign of Slammu.

As for Slammu, had he found a really slippery customer!

Having followed the suspicious figure, he found himself in one of the labs in the building. The figure had always remained one step ahead of him until they had gone into a hallway and the figure had turned a corner.

"Wait there! Wait there!"

The figure came back around the corner and looked straight at Slammu.

He was long and thin and had a small mouth that snapped open and shut rapidly. He had small beady eyes and his smooth and shiny skin was mottle brown.

"Who, may I ask, are you?" he hissed at the young shark.

"Big Slammu," said Slammu defiantly. "What are you doing here? Do you work for Dr. Piranoid?"

"Who is he?" replied the figure. "All I know is that one minute I was swimming around in a tank and the next I'm this large and three guys are bossing me about."

Slammu began to pity the figure. He himself knew what it was like to be changed suddenly into something else.

"Don't worry. We'll go and find my older brothers. They'll know what to do." This seemed to console the figure who allowed Slammu to put his arm around him and lead him down the hallway.

Down in the cellar the fight was getting quite heated with Slobster having Jab's arms in his pincers and Streex holding Slash in a head lock.

"Can't you get anything right?" shouted Piranoid as he continued to fire harpoons at Jab and Streex, but in his anger his aim had became very bad and the rockets went everywhere.

This excitement continued until suddenly one of the rockets hit the large water pipe in the room and water spumed out.

The room began to fill quickly with water and Piranoid, Slobster, Slash, Streex and Jab were washed away with the fast-moving water.

Streex let go of Slash as his body was flung against the basement wall. "Ooof! Blast it! I've let go of shell features." Streex was also flung against the basement wall, having had the rushing water aid his escape from Slash's hold.

"We had better get out of here, the place is filling with water!"

"I can't see Dr. Piranoid or the Seavites anywhere."

Streex and Jab tried to swim out of the basement towards the doorway, but the current was too strong even for the Shark brothers and they were pushed back into the room.

"Blast it, bro. How we gonna get out of here?" shouted Streex to his brother above the sound of rushing water.

At that moment on the far side of the room, Streex and Jab could just make out the shape of three figures being swept out of the other doorway Streex had come through.

"Looks like the bad guys are getting away!" shouted Streex.

"Blast it!" shouted Jab. "I'll get those salty cronies!"

Ripster, having noticed a large amount of water spilling out from the building and no sign of his brother Slammu, began rushing down the stairs to the cellar.

Slammu and his new friend had just made it to the reception area when they saw water gushing out of the lift shaft from the cellar.

49

Slammu looked at his friend. "Ah oh, looks like trouble, we'd better go and see." Slammu's friend looked a little nervous but trundled after Slammu, his large tail trailing behind him.

Streex and Jab could feel the water rising quite quickly and the strong current made them unable to move.

"Bro, I hate to say it, but I think this is it!" Streex shouted to Jab.

There was only a few feet of space left between the water and the ceiling. Both boys were trapped.

At the top of the stairs leading to the basement, Slammu could hear his brother's cries for help, but the rushing water kept pushing him back.

"I have to go and help them, but the water's too fast!"

Slammu's friend's feet were submerged in the rushing water and he began to gently lie his body over the water.

"What are you doing?" cried Slammu. "The water is too fast, you'll be swept away!"

"I can float on top of the waves," he replied. "I'll get your brothers for you."

Slammu was most surprised by his friend's offer of help but he knew it could be the only chance they had.

Slammu's friend's body was lithe and long and made a perfect surfboard shape on top of the water. He began to paddle furiously down into the cellar.

"Don't worry, bros!" cried Slammu. "A friend of mine is coming!"

There was now only two feet of space between the ceiling and the water.

Down in the cellar Jab and Streex were gripping hold of a pipe that became detached from the wall. The water was rushing by them quite quickly. They could hear their brother calling them from above, but his voice was quite faint above the sound of rushing water.

Above the water floated

Slammu's friend, paddling towards the **bros. He was just in time to grab Jab** before he slipped under the water and got washed away.

"Hey! Who are you?" spluttered Jab when he resurfaced.

"Your brother sent me to help you," replied the rescuer.

At the top of the stairs, Ripster had joined his brother Slammu.

"What's going on? Where are the others?"

Slammu pointed towards the rapidly increasing water that was now flooding both the stairway and the lift shaft, when suddenly a large rush of water came spouting out.

"Move some fin, bro, the water's doing a tidal!"

Both Slammu and Ripster ran out of the building into the street. It was still raining from that morning but it made no difference to the amount of water spuming out of the building.

Ripster and Slammu climbed on top of the Shark Cruiser to escape the rushing water.

the drain.

On top of the waves two figures could be seen, each in a surfing posture trying to balance on top of the waves.

"What a rush!" shouted Jab at

The water rolled out of the building as giant waves came crashing down the front steps, out on to the street and ran down the road forming giant puddles and a small stream into

the top of his voice.

Down the steps rode the surfing duo until the water had petered out and the boys had come to a gentle stop in front of the Shark Cruiser.

There on the ground was Slammu's friend with the two Shark brothers on his back. All three got up and Ripster and Slammu jumped off the top of the Cruiser. That's when the police sirens started.

"Looks like company, better move it!" suggested Ripster.

Slammu grabbed his friend and all the sharks zoomed off back to the comic shop.

Jab and Streex thanked their new friend for helping them out of the watery situation.

"So!" said Ripster. "You're a creation of Dr. Paradigm's as well."

Slammu's friend nodded. "If that's the guy with the eye patch, then yes."

"We're gonna have to hide him somewhere," muttered Slammu, worried that his new friend might fall into the clutches of Dr. Paradigm again.

Lena called to explain that she had found out what Dr. Paradigm's delivery had been: a giant conger eel from the coral reef, but she didn't know what he had done with it.

All four brothers sat down to think of what they could do for their friend.

"Giant conger eels don't blend in too well around here," sighed Slammu.

"Nor do sharks," replied Ripster.

Streex decided he'd had enough of thinking and began to preen himself at the mirror. The rain had stopped and he was going to check out the new shop assistant at the surf shop.

"That's it!" cried Ripster. "He can work at the surf shop!" All the brothers and their new friend stared at Ripster.

"What better place to hide a guy than out in the open? He can pretend to be an actor promoting surfing."

Streex suggested that the excess water had affected his brother's brain, worried that the new assistant may have another player for her affection.

Bends said he'd go and speak to the owner while Slammu suggested that they pay a visit to the burger bar as all that excitement had given him a hunger!

51

Dr. Paradigm ™

Age: No data
D.O.B: No data
Nationality: No data
Status: No data

Dr. Paradigm is the pillar of society, the people's hero, he is there when scientific answers are needed about major catastrophes, even if he may have caused them!

Eccentric and mad, he is a genius in his field, with Dr. Bolton being his only comparison.

Paradigm loves to play God and create new life forms which will be his slaves. His greatest creations are the Seavites who are submissive and strong but extremely stupid.

Having accidentally injected himself with piranha DNA, Paradigm changes dramatically into Piranoid when he loses his temper: a creature with sharp gnashing teeth and an attitude to match.

Paradigm blames everything that has happened to the Street Sharks on their father Dr. Bolton. He is searching desperately for Dr. Bolton's secret formula to help him create a super strong army of Seavites.

Paradigm's dearest wish is world domination and a submissive army of slaves, but unfortunately for him the Street Sharks stand in his way!

Slash™

Age: No data
Hobbies: Drilling and fighting
Fave food: Oysters and shark steaks

Slash is one of Dr. Piranoid's Seavites. A henchman and spy, he spends most of his time fulfilling the doctor's wishes and carrying out his diabolical plans.

Slash was created by bio-engineering a swordfish. Having no clear memory of his past as a normal swordfish, he has no real desire to go back to the sea, and no real desire to do anything else.

Slash hates the Street Sharks, especially Jab who always hurls insults at him.

Slash loves to bore through things with his diamond sharp nose and wishes that Slobster would think more for himself.

Slobster™

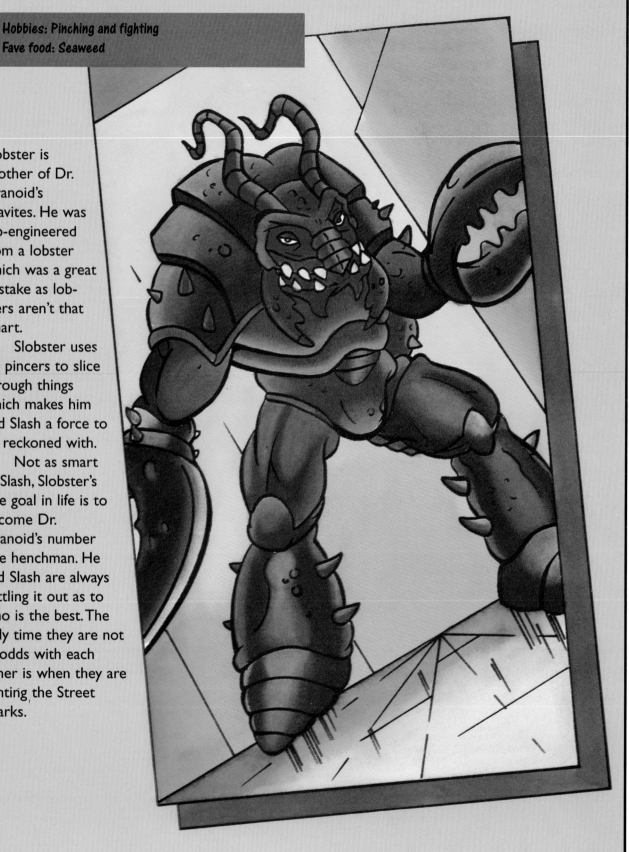

Hobbies: Pinching and fighting
Fave food: Seaweed

Slobster is another of Dr. Piranoid's Seavites. He was bio-engineered from a lobster which was a great mistake as lobsters aren't that smart.

Slobster uses his pincers to slice through things which makes him and Slash a force to be reckoned with.

Not as smart as Slash, Slobster's one goal in life is to become Dr. Piranoid's number one henchman. He and Slash are always battling it out as to who is the best. The only time they are not at odds with each other is when they are fighting the Street Sharks.

Prawn Cocktail To Go...

The boys were hanging out at the local burger bar and Ripster was pondering on why they had heard nothing from either Dr. Paradigm or the Seavites.

"It ain't good, guys. They're up to something, I can feel it in my lateral line!"

"You can feel everything down your lateral line, bro.' Loosen up, we'll hear from them soon enough," said Jab.

"Hey! Maybe the dudes have given up. Either that or they could have checked out of the city!"

Ripster stared at his brother Streex. He wondered if they really were brothers, having just come up with a stupid comment like that.

"No. These guys are never gonna give up without a fight. I know they're planning something, but what?"

Just at that moment Cindy the new waitress came up to the table. "Can I take your orders, guys?" she stammered nervously. The other girls had decided it was her turn to meet the bar's most toothy of customers.

"Yeah. Sweetheart, you can take my orders anyday," jeered Streex, giving a large toothy grin to the already nervous Cindy.

"Man, am I hungry..." muttered Slammu as he immersed himself in the menu, "...but there ain't anything here that will take the edge off my appetite."

"My appetite has just been whetted, with a little bit of honey," leered Streex at Cindy, who that moment had decided that turning down that job at the fishmonger's had been a bad idea.

Suddenly, Bends came whizzing round the corner on his latest invention: hover trainers with remote control. For the person who wants to

be somewhere else without having to change your footwear. "Hiya, guys, how's it hangin'?"

Slammu just waved his hand and muttered a hello. He was still immersed in the menu, Streex was trying not to take his eyes off Cindy (who was also doing the same with Streex but for a completely different reason) and Ripster was still pondering about Dr. Paradigm.

"Hiya, Bends. How's our business going?" said Jab.

"MMMmm. Jawsome, Jab, as ever. How are the burgers in this place? Any better than the last place?"

"Heh, it wasn't our faults the Seavites crashed the last place!"

Slammu's head popped up from the menu. "They did great anchovy pie there, you know." Slammu's head re-submerged into the menu.

"I'll have a prawn cocktail and glass of salt water. What about you, Ripster, heh?" said Jab. "It'll take your mind off things."

"Sorry, no prawn cocktail. The suppliers are all out of prawns since the robberies," said Cindy.

"What do you mean, no prawn cocktail? It's my fave," sighed Jab angrily.

"Wait a minute. What do you mean, robberies?" Ripster started up.

"It was in the newspapers, didn't you see? Someone's stealing all the prawns and no one knows why. That really great doctor guy, Dr. Paradigm, says it's the work of some students playing practical jokes. He's so great, don't you think? A real Doctor Guy."

"Sheesh Cindy, that hurt!" quipped Streex. "I'm much better than that guy, I can just roll right over that guy. Care to join me, sweet?"

Bends whizzed off to get a newspaper while Cindy decided it might be a lot safer if she went to serve the nice couple in the corner, much to Streex's distress.

"Here we go, guys," said Bends, opening the newspaper to an article entitled "Prawns on the run.."

"Ah hah! The forefront of journalism, better than last week's headline, Fish Fried At Local Burger Bar!" muttered Bends.

"Yeah, who said the Seavites were fish?" Jab was always pleased when he was able to poke fun at Dr Piranoid's henchmen.

The article explained that every local retailer had been robbed of his supply of prawns, leaving a great demand for prawns and an even greater mystery.

Dr. Paradigm had been quoted as saying that it was a local college fraternity prank and nothing to worry about. The Mayor had agreed, saying it wasn't worth bringing the police out for such a small fry of a problem.

"Well. Didn't I say Paradigm's up to something?" piped up Ripster. His brothers stared at him.

"You lost me, dude!" said Bends. "What's the guy up to, then?"

"Well, it's obvious. Why would Paradigm say that the thefts were nothing unless he has something to hide? He's covering up, he doesn't want to draw attention to the

robberies for some reason. And the Mayor's promised not to investigate. Whatever Paradigm's up to, he's quite safe for the moment."

"Well, there's only one thing to say to that, let's haul some fin!"

The guys agreed that they should hide out at the warehouse on the seafront. Bends had found out a delivery of prawns was due in from the Indian Ocean to fill the demand the thefts had left. Bends would stay at the workshop as back up to the Street Sharks and the brothers would hide and see who it was that was paying so much attention to the small crustaceans!

It was two in the morning and the cargo ship

had just delivered its load. The workmen had unloaded and left for home.

The place was deserted and the brothers were all in place when a rumbling sound started to come out of the ground. Suddenly, the sharp nose of a Driller vehicle came up through the floor.

"We know who owns that," whispered Ripster to Slammu. "We do!" said Slammu. "SSHHH, guys!" said Jab. "They'll hear us".

Out of the Driller's cab came Slobster and Slash, Dr. Piranoid's henchmen. They made quickly for the containers carrying the prawns and started to unload them into the Driller.

"Not so fast, Seaweed Breath!" shouted Jab as he jumped out of the shadows. "We want a word with you two!" joined in Streex.

Slobster and Slash dropped the boxes in surprise and dived back into the Driller's cab. "The boss ain't gonna be pleased with us!" said Slobster.

"Jam it shut, Slobster. If you hadn't got us lost, none of this would have happened" cursed Slash.

The engine of the Driller started up and the vehicle dived back into the ground.

"Well, we know who but we don't know why," said Streex to his older brother.

"Well, let's haul some fin and find out!" answered Ripster.

As the Driller drove into the ground the Street Sharks followed, their fins being the only visible part of them above the concrete as they swam through the ground to follow the Driller.

Back at the lab Dr. Paradigm was pacing the floor. He had sent his two felons out to get some fresh supplies and they had been gone for hours.

"Baah. Those two haven't got an intelligent cell between the two of them, let alone a brain. But when I have finished this experiment, I will have an army like no other. Indestructible, obedient and lots of them."

Paradigm turned to the large tank that was behind him. It was filled with hundreds and hundreds of prawns.

There was a slight whiff of cooked prawns in the air but Dr. Paradigm would have preferred you not to notice that. His last test to make his inde-structable army had resulted in a large fry for the small fry. Hence the need for Slobster and Slash to go and get some more prawns!

"This time it will work. Less heat and more sodium and then my army will be complete."

Suddenly, an alarm sounded in the lab. "Aha! That must be the crusty twins now, with my next batch of prawns."

Paradigm strode over to a console and looked at the screen. There were five bleeps blinking across it getting closer and closer to the lab.

"What? Those blithering idiots, what have they done now? If they've lead those sharks here, I'll batter and fry them!"

Dr. Paradigm got angrier and angrier, his face started to go purple with rage.

"Those idiots! Can they do nothing right?"

As Dr. Paradigm became more furious, a strange change came over him. His mouth began to fill with lots and lots of long, sharp teeth, his skin started to become yellow and his nose began to disappear. Where once Dr. Paradigm had stood now there stood Dr. Piranoid!

"I'm ready for those sharks now! I really fancy a bite or two!"

The nose of the Driller appeared through the docking bay and out jumped Slash and Slobster.

"Boss, Boss, we've got trouble. We bumped into the...." started Slash.

"I know, you blithering fools! You've lead the Street Sharks to my secret lab!"

Slash and Slobster looked from one to the other with horror on their faces, having suddenly realised what they had done.

"He drove, he did it!" said Slash pointing at Slobster, trying to blame the other Seavite and get himself out of trouble.

"Silence! Those sharks will be here soon, I'll turn on the radiation and turn the small fry we have now into an army. Getting rid of the Sharks will be a good first test for them!"

Piranoid faced the tank and began to flick a few switches and turn a few knobs. He quietly muttered to himself as he worked but the maniacal smile never left his face.

Slash and Slobster looked furiously around the lab trying to guess where the Street Sharks would surface.

All of a sudden, a humming sound began to erupt from the tank. "It will work, I know it will," muttered Piranoid.

The humming got louder and louder and the tank began to vibrate. Both Slash and Slobster stared at the tank where the water had begun to bubble and the prawns began to glow.

A fin suddenly emerged through the lab wall followed by another and another. Big Slammu's body came crashing through the wall and the young shark ran charging towards the two surprised Seavites.

"Seismic Slammin'!" shouted Slammu as he started to slam the floor of the lab with his fists.

Ripster, Streex and Jab shortly followed their brother into the lab and charged towards Piranoid who had decided to double the power to the prawn tank.

The seismic waves that Slammu created rocked the lab and sent Dr. Piranoid flying towards the Driller which he hit with his head and then fell to the ground.

Slobster and Slash were also sent flying, but they flew towards the large tank, their bodies hitting it with full impact. The tank's glass cracked and prawns began to tumble out.

Ripster charged towards Dr. Piranoid. "Time for a little action, I feel. Don't you agree, Toothy?"

"Blast you Sharks. Why can't you leave me alone? You're just like you're father, real busybodies!"

Dr Piranoid got to his feet and realised the tank of prawns was cracked. Large, glowing prawns were scattered on the floor and Slash and Slobster were buried underneath them.

"Blast it! My soldiers!" wailed Piranoid. He suddenly realised that he got the bump on the head from the Driller. He jumped into the cab and started the engine.

He had just slammed the door when Ripster and Streex jumped on to the Driller.

"Hold it, Dr. Death, we want a word with you!"

The engine of the Driller drowned out the Street Sharks' wails of protest as it dived into the ground through the floor of the lab.

"Piranoid! We'll get you!"

As the Driller disappeared into

the ground
the lab walls began to
shake even more.

"It looks like the lab's
coming down, the seismic waves must
have disturbed the foundation and the
Driller must have continued the
vibrations! We had better get out of
here before the ceiling comes in and
crushes us!" shouted Ripster above the
rumbling sound.

As Piranoid had made his escape
Jab and Slammu had come upon the
Seavites who were partially
hidden by enormous glowing shrimps.

"Get me out of here!" yelled
Slash.

Jab's eyes were nearly jumping
out of his head with the sight before
him.

There is nothing Jab likes more
apart from hurling insults at the

Seavites than to eat prawns.

Even before Jab was changed into
half a shark he loved prawns. Prawn
cocktail, prawn crisps, deep fried
prawns and boiled prawns. He just
loved prawns and the sight of the
large, juicy prawns scattering the lab
floor had Jab's mouth salivating.

"Drop it, Bro! We have got to go,
the lab walls are falling down!"

Streex had his hand on his
brother's shoulder and was trying to
pull him away from the mouthwatering
sight.

Jab opened his mouth and began
to stuff it full of the giant prawns with
his chompers. Chewing Jab had no
time for the two Seavites who decided

to follow their boss and
make a quick getaway. Jumping into
another Driller, they were off.

The second Driller's vibrations
made the lab walls shake even more
but Jab paid no notice to this and
continued to stuff his face.

"Let's go, guys, before it's too
late!" yelled Ripster who lead the way
through the tunnel the first Driller had
made to the lab.

Streex gave one final tug of his
brother's shoulder and then followed
Ripster out.

The Street Sharks began to swim
to the surface, their fins slowly
emerging through the concrete road at

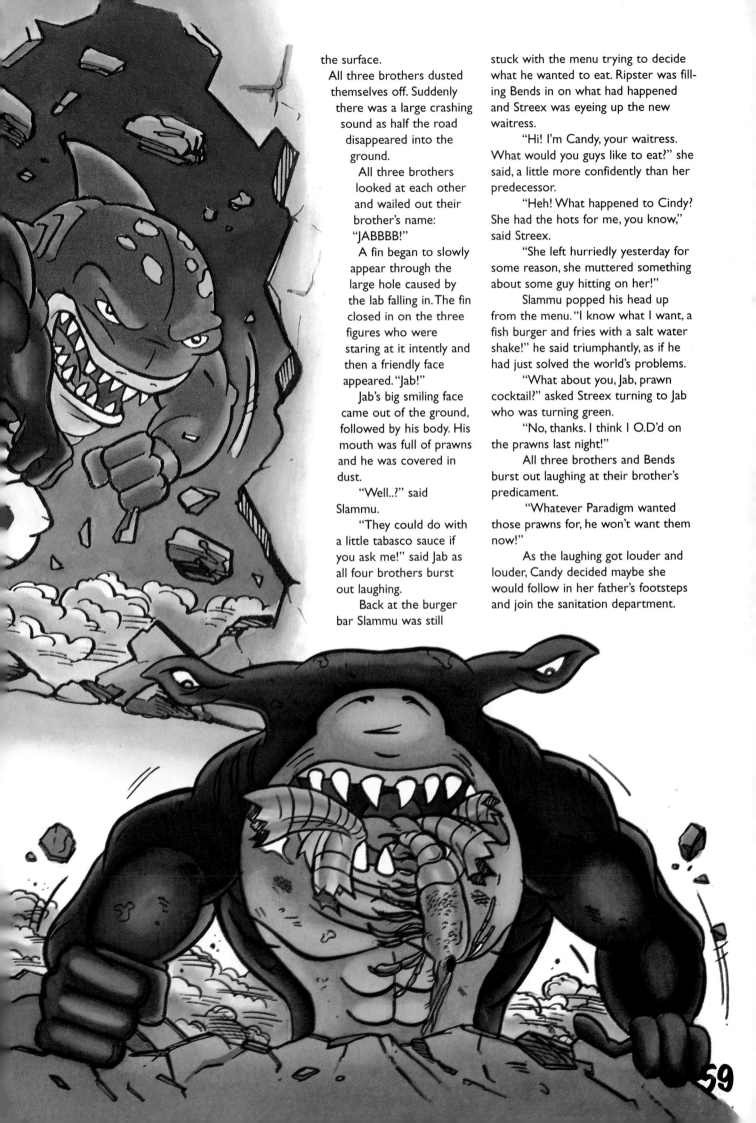

the surface.

All three brothers dusted themselves off. Suddenly there was a large crashing sound as half the road disappeared into the ground.

All three brothers looked at each other and wailed out their brother's name: "JABBBB!"

A fin began to slowly appear through the large hole caused by the lab falling in. The fin closed in on the three figures who were staring at it intently and then a friendly face appeared. "Jab!"

Jab's big smiling face came out of the ground, followed by his body. His mouth was full of prawns and he was covered in dust.

"Well..?" said Slammu.

"They could do with a little tabasco sauce if you ask me!" said Jab as all four brothers burst out laughing.

Back at the burger bar Slammu was still stuck with the menu trying to decide what he wanted to eat. Ripster was filling Bends in on what had happened and Streex was eyeing up the new waitress.

"Hi! I'm Candy, your waitress. What would you guys like to eat?" she said, a little more confidently than her predecessor.

"Heh! What happened to Cindy? She had the hots for me, you know," said Streex.

"She left hurriedly yesterday for some reason, she muttered something about some guy hitting on her!"

Slammu popped his head up from the menu. "I know what I want, a fish burger and fries with a salt water shake!" he said triumphantly, as if he had just solved the world's problems.

"What about you, Jab, prawn cocktail?" asked Streex turning to Jab who was turning green.

"No, thanks. I think I O.D'd on the prawns last night!"

All three brothers and Bends burst out laughing at their brother's predicament.

"Whatever Paradigm wanted those prawns for, he won't want them now!"

As the laughing got louder and louder, Candy decided maybe she would follow in her father's footsteps and join the sanitation department.

Colouring Page

Get your coloured markers or crayons out and add some colour to this action packed page.

ANSWER PAGES

Answers to page 16:
A creature that lays eggs BIRD
Throw it to get a number DICE
To go round and round SPIN
They are in the night sky STARS
Very big TALL
A large plant TREE
You run in it RACE

Answer: RIPSTER

Answers to page 17:
1) SLASH
2) RIPSTER
3) BRANDON BENDS-BANNER
4) LENA MACK
5) BIG SLAMMU
6) STREEX
7) J A B

Answers to page 18:

12	18	1	3	25
41	7	12	10	6
5	6	9	6	3
2	4	14	3	17
6	4	3	18	20

**ENTRY: E=5. N=14. T=20.
R=18. Y=25**

Answer to page 19:

Answer to page 24:

```
C Z V N E D D N A T T Y Y
A A A A A A V B S J R S M
A S R S B B A N N B K S E
Q W X R A J Q A O Q U R O
A A I W A J E A M L L A L
T H W A W A C S R R R S P
A B S S S J A J A B E B M
C Q W R X J V B M H G B T
N M R W J R Z G M K L O E
A J W L Q Z W J R R S S Z
F I A U Y A Y R L J U B A
U S R R J J V S X M N B A
Q R L R A R W C X A U I O
F J T Y W J W S S S R R O
A I I A X A E J A A A S P
H B J J R S I A J B B V W
C N A N S L K Y A M V C W
Q T K B Q A W R K M K B Y
A B R J R S A R S R R J L
L E M N Z A X S A A A B A
A B R A A R A Z A C V T K
I S O J A J L R J J S R A
U S P L R B Y Y T I J A Y
O J A Q A S U W Q J O I T
E E W A A E E J J B S S N
P A L N A R A T N M D D M
A A M A R A A S J J J R O
L B S J X X Y S U I P R Y
V W Q A R W Q R A R O R W
A L A E A J A B S J M J A
O I K M T O P U A O P N Q
```

Answers to page 25:
STREET SHARKS,
   BE CAREFUL DR. PARA-
DIGM IS LOOKING FOR YOU.
THE POLICE ARE HELPING
HIM.
   KEEP SAFE.
   FROM
   LENA MACK

Answer to page 46:

	TRUE	FALSE
TIGER SHARK	T	☐
RED SHARK	☐	F
ISLE OF WIGHT SHARK	☐	F
BLUE SHARK	T	☐
DOCTOR SHARK	☐	F
ELEPHANT SHARK	☐	F
HORSE SHARK	☐	F
NURSE SHARK	T	☐
RED NOSE SHARK	☐	F
WHALE SHARK	T	☐
PORT JACKSON SHARK	T	☐
SCREWDRIVER SHARK	☐	F
BLACK TIP SHARK	T	☐
DOLPHIN SHARK	☐	F
DEMON SHARK	☐	F
LEOPARD SHARK	T	☐
SMELLY SHARK	☐	F
ANGEL SHARK	T	☐
HORN SHARK	T	☐
HORSE SHARK	☐	F
BEACH SHARK	☐	F
LARGE SHARK	☐	F
SNAKE SHARK	☐	F
ZEBRA SHARK	T	☐
PUZZLE SHARK	☐	F
CROCODILE SHARK	T	☐

Answers to Trivia pages:

1. B	9. A	17. A
2. A	10. A	18. A
3. C	11. A	19. C
4. C	12. C	20. C
5. B	13. A	21. A
6. A	14. C	22. C
7. B	15. C	23. A
8. C	16. C	24. C

Answer to page 40:

```
A S L A S H E U W I Q D A S K D U W
R I P S T E R B N I I Q D A S K D S
S S D B K J E U W I Q D A S K B U L
L S D E K J E U A I Q D A S K I U A
O S D N K J E U W I Q D A S K G U M
B S D P K J E U W I Q D A S K D U M
S S D S K J E U R I S D A S K D U U
T S D H K J E U V I T D A S K D R W
E S D H K J D R P A R A D I G M U M
R S D H K J A B W D E A S K R U L L
A S D H K J E U M D E A S K D U E E
A S D H K J E U W I X D A S K D U M
D R B O L T O N W I Q M A C K D U A
```

61

COMPETITION

WIN THESE FANTASTIC STREET SHARKS PRIZES!

FIRST PRIZE: GLOW-IN-THE-DARK ACTION FIGURE
SECOND PRIZE: SHARK BIKE
THIRD PRIZE: HAND SHARK

All you have to do is answer these three simple questions:

1. Who owns Suspended Reality?

2. What is Slobster's favourite food?

3. What type of Shark is Streex?

Write your answers on a postcard or envelope with your name, age and address and send to:

Street Sharks Competition
Grandreams Limited
Jadwin House, 205-211 Kentish Town Road, London, NW5 2JU

Closing date for entries is March 31st 1997.

The first correct entry drawn out of the bag on the closing date will be awarded the Street Sharks action figure. The second correct entry will receive the shark bike and the third correct entry drawn will receive a hand shark. The publisher's decision is final and no correspondence will be entered into.